little Miss Tiny

by Roger Hargreaves

PSS!
PRICE STERN SLOAN
An Imprint of Penguin Group (USA) Inc.

Little Miss Tiny was extremely small.

Not very tall at all!

She was so very tiny she didn't live in a house.

Do you know where she lived?

In a mousehole, in the dining room of Home Farm.

She had made the mousehole quite comfortable really, and luckily there weren't any mice, because the farm cat had chased them all away.

The trouble was, because she was so tiny, nobody knew she lived there.

Nobody had noticed her.

Not even the farmer and his wife.

So, there she lived.

All alone.

With nobody to talk to.

She was very lonely.

And sad.

Oh, dear!

One day she was feeling so lonely, she decided to be very brave and go for a walk.

Out of her mousehole she came.

She crept across the dining room and went through the crack in the door and into the hall.

To Little Miss Tiny the hall looked as big as a field, and she scuttled across it to the back door of the farm.

Luckily for her the mail slot was at the bottom of the door, and she squeezed herself through it and onto the doorstep.

It was all very exciting.

There before her was the farmyard.

She went exploring.

She came to a door with a gap at the bottom, and ducked in underneath.

There, inside, was a pig.

A large pig!

And if you're as small as Little Miss Tiny, a large pig looks very large indeed.

Miss Tiny looked at the pig.

The pig looked at Miss Tiny.

"Oink," he grunted, and moved closer to inspect this little person who had entered his sty.

"Oh my goodness me," squeaked Little Miss Tiny in alarm, and shot out of the pigsty as fast as her little legs would carry her.

Which wasn't very fast because her legs were so very little!

She ran right around to the back of the pigsty before she stopped.

She leaned against the wall and put her hands over her eyes, and tried to get her breath back.

Suddenly, she heard a noise.

A very close noise.

A sort of breathing noise.

Very close indeed!

Oh!

She hardly dared take her hands away from her eyes, but when she did she wished she hadn't.

What do you think it was, there, right in front of her, looking at her with green eyes?

Ginger!

The farm cat!!

Poor Little Miss Tiny.

Ginger grinned, showing his teeth.

"HELP!" shrieked Little Miss Tiny at the top of her voice. "Oh somebody please HELP!"

The trouble was, the top of Little Miss Tiny's voice was not a very loud place.

Ginger grinned another grin.

Every day Mr. Strong went to Home Farm to buy some eggs.

He liked eggs.

Lots of them.

That day he was walking home across the farmyard when he heard a very tiny squeak.

He stopped.

There it was again.

Around the corner.

He looked around the corner and saw Ginger and the poor trapped Little Miss Tiny.

"SHOO!" said Mr. Strong to Ginger, and picked up Little Miss Tiny.

Very gently.

"Hello," he said. "Who are you?"

"I'm...I'm...I'm...Little Miss Tiny."

"You are, aren't you?" smiled Mr. Strong. "Well, if I were as tiny as you, I wouldn't go wandering around large farmyards!"

"But..." said Little Miss Tiny, and told Mr. Strong about how she was so lonely she had to come out to find somebody to talk to.

"Oh, dear," said Mr. Strong. "Well now, let's see if we can't find you some friends to talk to."

So now, every week, Mr. Strong comes to get Little Miss Tiny and takes her off to see her friends.

Three weeks ago he took her to see Mr. Funny, who told her so many jokes she just couldn't stop laughing all day.

Two weeks ago he took her to see Mr. Greedy.

He told her his recipe for his favorite meal.

"But that's much too much for tiny little me," she laughed.

Mr. Greedy grinned.

"For you," he said, "divide the measurements by a hundred!"

Last week Mr. Strong took her to see Mr. Silly.

And Mr. Silly showed her how to stand on her head.

"That's very silly," giggled Little Miss Tiny.

"Thank you," replied Mr. Silly, modestly.

And guess whom she met this week?

Somebody who's become a special little friend.

Mr. Small.

"I never thought I'd ever meet anybody smaller than myself," laughed Mr. Small.

Little Miss Tiny looked up at him, and smiled.

"You wait till I grow up," she said.